♥ Eva's Treetop Festival ♥

Rebecca
Elliott

SCHOLASTIC

For Clementine. My wide-eyed
little night owl. — R.E.

Special thanks to Eva Montgomery.

Scholastic Children's Books
An imprint of Scholastic Ltd
Euston House, 24 Eversholt Street, London, NW1 1DB, UK
Registered office: Westfield Road, Southam, Warwickshire, CV47 0RA
SCHOLASTIC and associated logos are trademarks and/or
registered trademarks of Scholastic Inc.

First Published in the US by Scholastic Inc, 2015
First published in the UK by Scholastic Ltd, 2015

ISBN 978 1407 15582 1

A CIP catalogue record for this book
is available from the British Library.

Printed and bound in Italy
Papers used by Scholastic Children's Books are made
from wood grown in sustainable forests.

3 5 7 9 10 8 6 4 2

www.scholastic.co.uk

♥ Table of Contents ♥

♡ Meet Eva ♡

Tuesday

Hello Diary,
   My name is Eva Wingdale. I live at Treehouse 11 on Woodpine Avenue in Treetopolis.

<u>I love</u>:
YOU – my new diary!

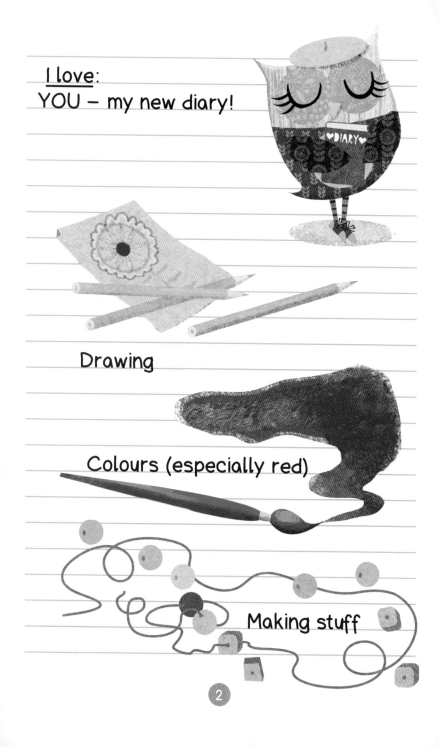

Drawing

Colours (especially red)

Making stuff

2

The word <u>pumpkin</u>

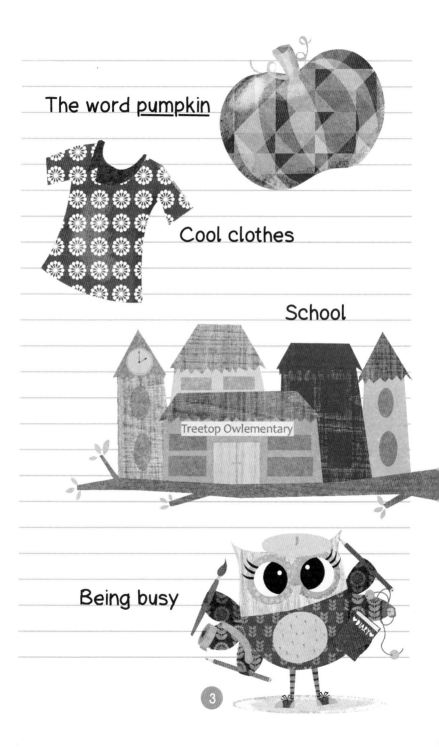

Cool clothes

School

Treetop Owlementary

Being busy

<u>I DO NOT love</u>:

My brother Humphrey's
stinky socks

Sue Clawson
(She is REALLY mean!)

Cleaning my beak

The word <u>plop</u>

PLOP

8+2=?

Asking for help

Squirrels

Mum's slug sandwiches

Being bored

5

Owls are super cool.

We're awake in the night-time.

We're asleep in the daytime.

We can turn our heads almost all the way around.

And we can fly!

Here is my owl family:

Me

Dad

the Wingdales

Baby Mo

Humphrey

Mum

AND here is my pet bat, Baxter!

He's so cute!

My very BEST friend in the whole **OWLIVERSE** is Lucy Beakman.

Lucy lives in the tree next door to mine. We have sleepovers all the time!

Lucy also sits next to me at school. Here is a photo of our class:

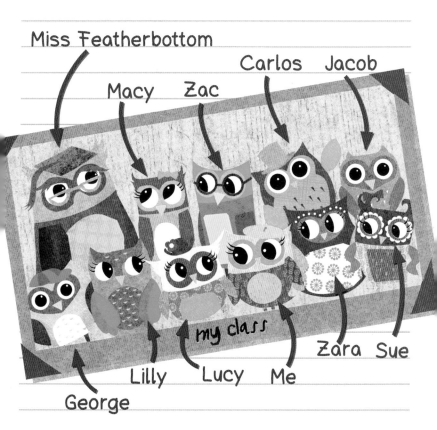

Miss Featherbottom

Carlos   Jacob

Macy   Zac

my class

Zara   Sue

Lilly   Lucy   Me

George

Oh, no! I'm late for school! I'll write again tomorrow, Diary.

♥ Bored, Bored, BORED! ♥

Wednesday

When I got home from school today, I did the same things I always do.

I took Baxter for a fly.

I ate a snack.

I did my **WINGLISH** homework.

I did arts and crafts.

I made this cool
bead bracelet!

I tried on new outfits.

I had a fight with Humphrey. He left his stinky socks in my bedroom AGAIN! He is such a squirrel-head!

But after all that, I still had HOURS to go before sunrise. I had <u>nothing</u> to do!

I called Lucy.

Lucy! I am <u>SO</u> bored! Can you come over?

Sorry! I can't. Tomorrow is the first day of spring, so my mum and I are planting flowers.

Flowers? Spring?! Lucy, you are a genius!

Huh? I am? OK, then!

Gotta go!

Bye, Eva!

Thank goodness for Lucy! She just gave me the most **FLAPPY-FABULOUS** idea!! I need to brainstorm! I'll be back!

OK, Diary. I've been thinking and thinking. Now I have the BEST plan <u>ever</u>! But there is no time to tell you. I'm off to bed. I cannot wait to tell Lucy (and YOU) all about it tomorrow!

3

♡ Miss Featherbottom ♡

Thursday

Hi Diary,

   I told Lucy about my big plan on our flight to school tonight.

Bloomtastic Festival

Lucy really liked my idea.

Wow, Eva, that sounds flap-tastic! When will you ask Miss Featherbottom about it?

Tonight. But I'm a bit scared she won't like my idea.

Oh, Eva! She'll LOVE it! It sounds like a lot of work. But it is a great idea!

I went to see Miss Featherbottom, our teacher, as soon as I got to class.

We always celebrate holidays in our classroom, but I was thinking... Because today is the first day of spring, our class could have a spring festival! And I'd like to organize it, if that's OK?

Miss Featherbottom didn't say anything. So I kept talking. I told her about the contests and the prizes.

The festival would be called the Bloomtastic Festival. Because spring is when flowers come out — or, um, bloom. This festival would be ALL about flowers!

Finally, Miss Featherbottom smiled.

A spring festival is a fabulous idea, Eva! What a hoot! And, yes, you may be in charge. But please, dear, don't take on too much yourself. Share the work.

Oh, and the festival can be next Thursday. We will give out your prizes next Friday.

Uh-oh, Diary. Next Thursday is only a week away! How will I get everything done in time?!

But I'm just SO very happy that Miss Featherbottom liked my idea!

YAY!

I told Lucy everything right before class.

Lucy, guess what! Miss Featherbottom loved my idea!

That's flaperrific, Eva!

But I have only <u>seven</u> days to get everything ready! Where do I start?

Make a to-do list. Then you'll know what you need to get done.

Lucy is the best friend EVER. She always knows what to do.

As soon as I got home, I wrote my to-do list:

1. Paint the set for the talent show

2. Set up tables for the bake-off

3. Hang frames for the art show

4. Build the runway for the fashion show

5. Make prizes

This is a great, long list! I know one thing, Diary: I won't be bored anymore! YAY! I'm off to sleep now. Good day!

♡ Meany McMeanerson ♡

Tonight was NOT a good night.

First, Miss Featherbottom told our class about the festival.

The Bloomtastic Festival will be next Thursday! There will be <u>four</u> contests for you to enter. And I will be giving out prizes next Friday.

Then she asked me to come up front.
I was a bit nervous as I flew up there.

I told everyone how the festival is all
about flowers. Then I told them where
to sign up for the contests.

Everything was going well.

BUT THEN, Sue Clawson said
something really bossy.

My wings got all shaky. Everyone was looking at me. I did not like it.

I'm in charge of the festival because ... uh ... it was my idea. And I want everyone to have fun. I don't want anyone else to have to worry about getting things ready.

Well, I should be in charge of the fashion show. My mum is a fashion designer!

I've got that taken care of. But thank you, Sue.

I flew back to my seat.

Sue is always sticking her beak into my business. And she is always SO mean. Her name <u>should be</u> Meany McMeanerson.

MEANY
McMEANERSON
100555

One time Sue told me my mum makes stinky sandwiches. (This is true, but she still shouldn't have said it.)

Then Miss Featherbottom
stood up.

Settle down, everyone.
I'm sure Eva will ask for some
help. And I want you <u>all</u> to have
Sue's excellent, helpful attitude!
You're setting a wonderful
example, Sue. Thank you.

After I organize this amazing festival,
I hope Miss Featherbottom will say
something nice like that about me, too.

Wait, Diary! My night got even worse after that! Sue walked over to me at lunch.

Good luck building the runway on your own, Eva. You're going to need it!

Argh! Meany McMeanerson is <u>such</u> a meany!

Before bed, I tried not to think about what Sue had said. I'm sure I can build a great runway. Right, Diary?

Now I'm worrying about everything I have to do for the festival. This will be a busy weekend!

Sleep tight, Diary!

5

♡ Practice Makes Perfect ♡

Saturday

Today, I started to paint the talent show set.

Lucy came over to keep me company — and to work on her contest entries. Since I am planning the festival, I won't be entering the contests. So I wanted to help Lucy!

I gave her my yummiest cupcake recipe for the bake-off.

Eva's Scrummy Cupcakes

1 cup birdseed
1 cup flour
1 cup acorns
2 slugs

- Mix everything together
- Bake for 20 minutes
- Let cupcakes cool
- Put loads of icing on top
- Enjoy!

I promised to help her bake after school on Wednesday. That way, her cupcakes will be super-fresh for Thursday's contest.

Next, I helped Lucy choose an outfit for the fashion show.

Then she painted a picture of her pet lizard, Rex, for the art show. That was such a **HOOT**!

I drew a picture of Baxter wearing a bunny costume, too.

Just before bed, I helped Lucy practise some dance moves for the talent show.

Baxter really liked our moves!

Humphrey did not.

Ha! You two look like a couple of crazy flamingoes doing the cha-cha!

He is such a squirrel-head.

I didn't finish painting the set today. But I have all day tomorrow. So don't worry, Diary. **ANYHOOT**, this festival is going to be great!

♥ Time Flies! ♥

Sunday

Hi Diary,
   I'm awake super-early!

   I haven't finished the talent show set
yet, but I want to start building the
runway today. (I'll show Sue that I can
do this on my own!)

I also have to make the prizes for the festival – they're going to be <u>SO</u> amazing!

Eva!

Uh-oh. Mum's calling me. I'll be back, Diary.

I'm back!

Humphrey and I spent the night with Granny Owlberta and Grandpa Owlfred!

Granny

Grandpa

It was great to see them. But it's almost daytime already! I haven't got anything done! EEK! And now the phone is ringing!

Lucy called to see how I'm doing with my to-do list.

Not great, Lucy! I've just been so busy!

Feathering flaps, Eva! The Bloomtastic Festival is only four days away! Are you sure you don't want <u>an</u>y help?

Thanks, Lucy, but I still think I'll be OK.

Time flew this weekend! Sorry I can't write more, Diary. But I have to make the prizes before bed. Gotta fly! Bye!

♥ Too-Hoo Much to Do ♥

Arrrghhhhhhhh!!!

The festival is only THREE DAYS AWAY!

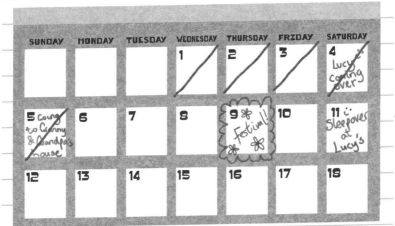

I've been so busy helping Lucy and creating the best prizes EVER that nothing else is ready! (But the prizes are finished. And I can't wait for everyone to see how cool they look!)

Diary, you know I wanted to do this festival all on my own. But I need some help — a LOT of help.

I'm going to talk to Lucy after school. I'll write more later!

Lucy was a BIG help. Well, sort of.

We painted half of the talent show set. But our wings got tired.

We tried to hang the frames for the art show. But we couldn't reach!

We planned a flower-shaped table design for the bake-off. But we didn't start building the table.

We even started building the runway. But it's a really big job!

So we have <u>A LOT</u> left to do:

1. Finish painting the talent show set

2. Hang the frames for the art show

3. Build the flower-shaped table for the bake-off

4. Finish building the runway for the fashion show

Lucy, I just don't have enough wings to do everything.

Don't worry, Eva. We'll figure something out.

Oh, Diary! Will I have to cancel the festival?

♡ A Helping Wing ♡

Tuesday

When I woke up today, I thought about how sad everyone would be if we cancelled the festival.

Then I thought about what Miss Featherbottom had said when I first told her my idea.

Share the work!

Finally, Diary! I know what I have to do! I was so silly to think that I could do ALL of this work on my own. NO ONE could! There are so many talented owls in my class. I just have to ask for help! Wish me luck, Diary! I'll write again after school.

I thought about who was good at what in my class. Then I asked my classmates to help with the part of the festival they'd be best at. To my surprise, everyone actually <u>wanted</u> to help! We all had fun together, too!

George, Carlos and Zara are the best painters in the class. So I asked them to paint the talent show set.

Zac and Macy are the tallest owls in the class. So I asked them to hang the frames for the art show.

Lilly and Jacob are good at building things. So I asked them to make the table for the bake-off. They loved Lucy's and my flower design!

I still need help with the runway. But Sue was out today. (She had to go to the **OWLADONTIST**!) I must ask for her help tomorrow. But I'm SO nervous.

Lucy, I'm scared of asking Sue for help. What if she laughs at me? What if she says something mean? Or what if she says no?

There's no way to know what Sue will say. Just be the lovely, fluffy, hoot of an owlet that you are and see what happens.

But tomorrow is the day before the festival. If Sue says no and the runway is not ready, we'll have to cancel the fashion show!!!!

9

♥ An Odd Day ♥

Wednesday

I spoke to SUE!! Here is what happened:

I could not believe that Sue said yes. She even smiled at me. Kind of.

Then she helped me build the runway after school.

Later, Lucy came over. We baked her cupcakes for the bake-off contest. And we made a flower on top of each cupcake!

After we made flower cupcakes, we had a flour fight! It was really fun!

It's been an odd day. But a good one. And I cannot believe that <u>TOMORROW</u> is the BIG day, Diary!! EEK!

♡ The Festival ♡

Thursday

Hello Diary,
   Today's festival was
a huge success
for everyone...

60

Just not for me. I spent the day running around to make sure everything was going OK. But everything went wrong.

First, Lucy's cupcakes did not look like pretty flowers. We had frosted the cupcakes when they were still hot. The frosting melted. And now they looked like gloopy SNOT balls!

Next, I saw that my just-for-fun painting of Baxter had been hung up in the art show! Lucy's was nowhere to be seen. She must've turned in my painting by mistake. Oh, Lucy! No one was supposed to see mine! Baxter looked like a <u>CRAZY ALIEN!</u>

Later, at the talent show, I tripped and landed on Miss Featherbottom!

Um. Hope you're enjoying the show!

The fashion show was the last contest. And I walked out onstage with my dress tucked into my <u>underpants</u>!!

ARGH! The whole festival was so **FEATHER-FLAPPINGLY** embarrassing! I'm sure everyone thinks I'm a total squirrel-head.

After Miss Featherbottom gives out the contest prizes tomorrow, I hope that I <u>never</u> have to hear about this festival again!

11

♥ Blooming Fabulous! ♥

I went to class early to drop off the contest prizes.

Then I tried to hide from everyone.

Miss Featherbottom started **HOOTING**:

The first Bloomtastic Festival was truly fabulous! Now, I will announce the contest winners...

Best painting

Talent show winner

Best cupcakes

Best outfit

Everyone liked the prizes I made. (I felt bad that Lucy didn't win. I never should have helped her with those cupcakes!)

Then, Miss Featherbottom asked me to come up front. I thought she was going to **SCREECH** at me for showing my underpants! But instead ...

... she gave me a special prize!

Thank you, Eva, for working so hard and for getting the whole class to work together! We couldn't have had this amazing festival without you.

I was <u>so</u> happy! But I knew that it wouldn't be right to take the prize.

Best Spring Festival Organizer

I'm sorry, but I cannot accept this trophy.

Can all of my classmates come up here, please?

My classmates flew up front. Lucy stood next to me.

This festival never would have happened without the help of all of you.

Best Spring Festival Organizer

We all took turns holding the trophy. Miss Featherbottom smiled. Everyone **HOOTED** and cheered! Even Sue!

Diary, it was the best feeling ever.

Now I just need to think of my next project!

Hmm... How soon can I start planning a summer festival?

Rebecca Elliott was a lot like Eva when she was younger: She loved making things and hanging out with her best friends. Now that Rebecca is older, not much has changed — except that her best friends are her husband, Matthew, and their children Clementine, Toby and Benjamin. She still loves making things, like stories, cakes, music and paintings. But as much as she and Eva have in common, Rebecca cannot fly or turn her head all the way around. No matter how hard she tries.

Rebecca is the author of JUST BECAUSE and MR SUPER POOPY PANTS. OWL DIARIES is her first early chapter-book series.

OWL DIARIES

How much do you know about Eva's Treetop Festival?

Name some cool owl facts.

Eva creates the word <u>bloomtastic</u>. This word is made up of two real words: <u>bloom</u> and <u>fantastic</u>. What do you think <u>bloomtastic</u> means?

Does Eva think the festival is a success? Why or why not?

How does Eva feel about me at the beginning of the story and at the end? What does Eva learn about teamwork?

Would you want to take part in the fashion show, talent show, art show or bake-off? Use words and pictures to describe what you would do.

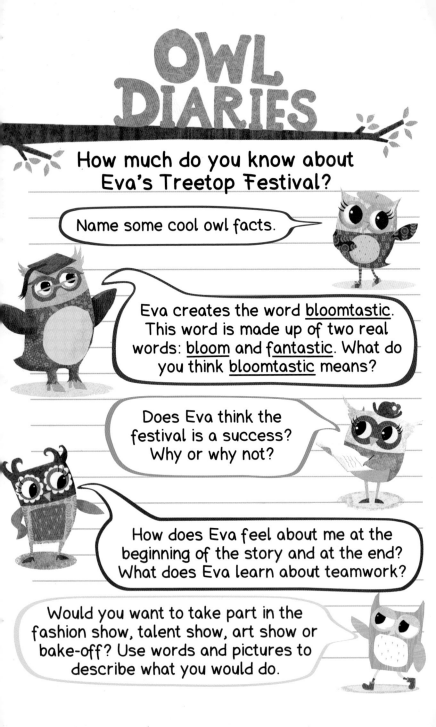